Halloween
Fraidy-Cat

by ABBY KLEIN

illustrated by
JOHN MCKINLEY

THE BLUE SKY PRESS
An Imprint of Scholastic Inc. • New York

To Toes and Schmoop:
My favorite trick-or-treaters.
Happy Haunting!
Love, A. K.

THE BLUE SKY PRESS

Text copyright © 2006 by Abby Klein
Illustrations copyright © 2006 by John McKinley
All rights reserved.

Special thanks to Robert Martin Staenberg.

No part of this publication may be reproduced, stored in
a retrieval system, or transmitted in any form or by any means,
electronic, mechanical, photocopying, recording, or otherwise,
without written permission of the publisher. For information
regarding permission, please write to: Permissions Department,
Scholastic Inc., 557 Broadway, New York, New York 10012.
SCHOLASTIC, THE BLUE SKY PRESS, and associated logos are
trademarks and/or registered trademarks of Scholastic Inc.
Library of Congress catalog card number:2006002228
ISBN 0-439-78457-3
10 9 8 7 6 5 4 3 2 1   06 07 08 09 10
Printed in the United States of America   40
First printing, August 2006

CHAPTERS

I have a problem.

A really, really, big problem.

I have been invited to

a Halloween party. I love

Halloween, but I'm scared

of all the ghosts, goblins,

and monsters!

Let me tell you about it.

CHAPTER 1

You're Invited

"Guess what, everyone?" Chloe said excitedly, as the class sat down to lunch. "Next Saturday I am going to have a big Halloween party, and you're all invited!"

"Cool!" Max said. "That sounds like fun, even if it is at *your* house."

"That's not a very nice thing to say, Max. I'm not going to invite you now unless you say you're sorry."

"B-b-but . . ." Max stammered. Chloe got

on his nerves, but he really wanted to go to the party. Chloe lived in a huge house, and she always had the best parties.

"I'm waiting," Chloe said with one hand cupped behind her ear. "What do you have to say to me, Maxwell?"

Max's face turned bright red. He hated being called Maxwell.

"I'm sorry," Max mumbled.

"What's that? I didn't hear you," said Chloe. "You need to speak up." She was really enjoying acting like the teacher.

"SORRY!" he barked in her face.

"Well, you don't have to yell," Chloe said as she shrank back. I think she realized she was starting to make Max angry, and that was definitely not something anybody wanted to do. After all, he was the biggest bully in the whole first grade.

"OK, you can come, but don't get any slime or fake blood on my new pink satin gown," Chloe said. "My mom had someone sew it just for me because there wasn't one I liked at the costume store."

"Let me guess," Jessie said. "You're going to be a princess for Halloween."

"Yes! How did you know?" Chloe chirped.

"A lucky guess," Jessie couldn't help muttering. "Personally, I think you should be the Bride of Frankenstein."

"Ewww," Chloe said, wrinkling up her nose. "That's not very pretty, and besides, I would never be married to a monster, only Prince Charming."

"Whatever, Cinderella. I wouldn't be caught dead wearing pink," said Jessie. "I'm going to be Dracula. I've already got the bloody fangs."

"Girls can't be Dracula," Max said, laughing.

"Why not?" asked Jessie.

"Because that's a boy's costume."

"No it's not."

"Yes it is."

"Says who?"

"Says me."

"Well, you're wrong. The great thing about Halloween is that you can dress up as anything you want. Right, Freddy?"

"Uh, yeah, right," I said. "I think Jessie is going to be a great Dracula. I can't wait to see her in her costume. I bet it's going to be really scary. You know Jessie's not afraid of anything."

"And how about you, wimp?" Max said, turning his attention to me. "What are you going to be this year? Wait, let me guess. Some kind of shark?"

"What makes you think I'm going to be a shark?"

"Uh, duh, because you dress up as one every year!" said Max, twirling his right pointer finger to make the cuckoo sign.

"Freddy is not crazy," said Jessie. "He just really likes sharks. Is there anything wrong with that?"

"No, it's just so boring to be the same thing every year," Max said.

I do really love sharks. They are my favorite animal on the planet. I dress up as a different kind of shark each year for Halloween. Last year I was a thresher shark, but the long tail sort of got in my way. This year I was thinking of wearing a hammerhead costume. I hadn't actually decided for sure yet.

"Well, Max, for your information," Robbie interrupted, "Freddy is a different *kind* of shark every year. All sharks are not the same, you know." Robbie is my best friend, and he is like a science genius. He knows everything about everything.

"Whatever, geek," Max shot back. "You all are so boring."

"Oh yeah?" said Jessie. "What are you dressing up as, Max? A ballerina?" Everyone at the table started to crack up. I was laughing so hard I thought my milk was going to come out of my nose. The thought of Max in a pink leotard and tutu was hilarious.

"Ha-ha," said Max, "very funny, but no."

"A bunny rabbit with whiskers and a little cottontail?" Jessie continued.

Now I was laughing uncontrollably. I almost fell off the bench I was sitting on, and some chewed-up bologna came flying out of my mouth. Jessie was so brave to always stand up to Max. I wish I were that brave.

"Oh, that's so funny, I forgot to laugh," Max said. Then he narrowed his eyes. "If you wimps really want to know, I am going to be a zombie. My costume is going to scare the pants off all of you guys."

"What do you mean?" Chloe squeaked. "How scary is it?" I could tell she was starting to think twice about inviting Max to her Halloween party.

"It was the scariest costume in the store."

I wasn't sure *I* wanted to hear about Max's costume, or see it for that matter. I was really afraid of ghosts, goblins, and monsters of any kind. Just seeing them gave me nightmares,

but I didn't want to say that, or everybody would think I was a baby. "Oh, yeah, what makes it so scary?" I said, trying to sound as tough as possible.

"It has this pump inside," Max continued, "that pumps fake blood. If I squeeze the handle, it looks like blood is dripping down my body. It is so cool, and the blood looks real. The mask is really scary, too. When I tried it on in the costume store, some little girl started crying."

I gulped. That really did sound scary. I thought if I saw it, I might have nightmares for months.

"It doesn't sound that scary," Jessie said. "Besides, we know the blood is fake."

"Right," I thought to myself. "Now, just remember the blood is fake."

"Well, we'll see how brave you all are next Saturday," said Max.

"I can't wait," said Jessie. "I'll be laughing, not crying."

"Yeah, laughing," I mumbled, smiling weakly. Maybe I could get the chicken pox by next Saturday, and then no one would know what a fraidy-cat I really was.

CHAPTER 2

Fraidy-Cat

"Freddy, honey, you got some mail today," my mom said as she handed me a bright orange envelope.

"Did I get one?" Suzie asked.

"No. Sorry, honey. Just Freddy."

"That's not fair!" Suzie whined.

"What do you mean it's not fair?" my dad asked. "Your mother and I do not work at the Post Office. We don't control the mail."

"Let me see it," Suzie said, trying to grab the envelope out of my hand. "Who's it from?"

"Suzie," my dad said, "that is Freddy's mail, not yours. Stop trying to grab it."

"Well, I just want to know who it's from," she insisted.

"Freddy will tell you as soon as he opens it," my mom said. "Just be patient a minute."

"Oh, I don't need to open it. I already know who it's from," I said.

"Do you have special powers?" my mom asked. "How do you know who it's from?"

"It's from Chloe."

"Chloe?" Suzie said. "You don't even like her. What would she be inviting you to?"

"She's having a big Halloween party, and she invited the whole class. She told us about it at lunch today."

"Well, I guess we know who won't be going," Suzie teased.

"Why wouldn't Freddy go?" my mom asked.

"Why wouldn't he go? Why wouldn't he go? Are you kidding me, Mom?" Suzie said.

"Yeah, Suzie," said my dad. "Why wouldn't Freddy go to a Halloween party?"

"Because he is only the biggest fraidy-cat on the whole planet," Suzie continued. "He can't even *look* at pictures of monsters without having nightmares."

"I can, too!" I butted in.

"Oh no you can't," said Suzie. "The last time you saw that movie poster with the zombies on it, you had nightmares for weeks!"

"Well, even tough guys get scared once in a while," said my dad, winking at me.

"And besides, Freddy's getting to be a big boy," said my mom. "I think he's old enough

22

to go to a Halloween party and not have nightmares."

"Oh yeah, right," Suzie snickered.

I opened the envelope and looked at the invitation. There was a spooky haunted house on the front, and above the house it said, "Come to our haunted house if you dare. You'll have a ghoul of a good time!"

"See, what did I tell you?" said Suzie. "It's going to be a haunted house." Then she made her voice sound spooky. "And in a spooky haunted house, there are ghosts, and goblins, and monsters that jump out at you." Then she jumped at me and yelled, "BOO!"

I leaped about ten feet in the air.

Suzie started laughing hysterically. "That

was one of the funniest things I ever saw. You are such a fraidy-cat, Freddy."

"Suzie, that was not very nice," said my mom. "You didn't need to scare him like that."

"Scare him! All I did was yell 'Boo!' If he was afraid of that, there is no way the little baby can go to this party without his mommy and daddy."

"Moms and dads aren't invited," I interrupted. "It's for kids only."

"Then you'd better call and tell them you won't be coming."

"Suzie, that is enough," my dad said. "Unless you have something encouraging to say to your brother, I would like you to keep your mouth shut."

"B-but . . ." Suzie stammered.

"I mean it," said my dad. "Or else I'll send you to your room."

"The party sounds really fun. Chloe was talking about it at school today, and everyone's going," I said, trying not to sound nervous about it even though I was.

"I know you've been scared of some Halloween creatures," said my mom, "but I bet they don't scare you anymore. I think you are old enough now to go by yourself."

"Of course I'm old enough to go, Mom. I'm not afraid of those things. I'm not a baby," I said, still trying to convince myself.

Suzie started to open her mouth again, but my dad glared at her, so she closed it and didn't say anything.

"That's right," said my dad. "There's nothing to be afraid of."

"I know the blood is fake, and the monsters are just dolls or people dressed up in scary costumes."

"Exactly," said my dad.

"When is the party?" my mom asked.

"Next Saturday."

"Next Saturday! That's only a week away. We'd better get started on your costume."

"I was thinking that this year I would be a hammerhead, Mom."

"Ugh," Suzie moaned. "A shark! Are you ever going to dress up as something else?"

"What difference does it make to you, Suzie?" my dad asked.

"It's just that there are so many cool costumes at the party store. I thought that one year Freddy might wear something that didn't embarrass me. Those shark costumes are just so lame."

"I beg your pardon, young lady," said my mom, "but I work very hard on those special shark costumes."

Because I can't find any shark costumes in the store, every year my mom makes my costume for me.

"Don't get me wrong, Mom," Suzie continued. "You do a great job. But I mean, who dresses up as a shark? Halloween is a time for ghosts, and monsters, and ninjas."

"Halloween is a time to dress up as your favorite thing, and Freddy loves sharks. Why shouldn't he dress up as one?"

"One year I could understand, but *every* year? Do me a favor, just look at the other costumes this year, OK?" said Suzie.

"Fine, I'll look," I said. Maybe she had a point. Maybe I wouldn't be so afraid of the monsters if I dressed up as one. I could remind myself that it was just a person in a costume like me.

"Well, since the party is next weekend,

I'd better take you two to the party store tomorrow," my mom said.

"Cool," said Suzie. "I hope they still have the Bride of Frankenstein costume I want to wear this year."

"Yeah, cool," I mumbled, faking a smile. I was already starting to feel a little queasy about seeing those monster masks staring down at me from the party store wall.

CHAPTER 3

It's Just a Mask!

The next day after school, my mom took Suzie and me to the party store to pick out costumes. As we pulled up, Suzie pointed out the window and yelled, "Oooo . . . look! That is the coolest costume ever!"

In front of the store, there was a guy dressed in a zombie costume carrying a sign that read "The Best Costumes in Town!"

"Freddy, isn't that a cool costume?" Suzie said. "Maybe you want to be that this year."

I wasn't even sure if I wanted to get out of the car. That thing was really scary. I had to look away.

"Uh, Earth to Freddy. Earth to Freddy," Suzie said, waving her hand in front of my face.

"What?"

"I said, isn't that a cool costume that guy is wearing? Don't you want to be that this year instead of some dumb old shark?"

"Yeah, maybe," I said, smiling weakly. Who was I kidding? I wouldn't put that costume on if you paid me a million bucks! It was way too scary. I wouldn't even be able to look at myself in the mirror.

My mom stopped the car, and Suzie jumped out. I didn't move. I was still trying to talk myself into getting out of the car. "It's just a guy in a costume," I mumbled to myself. "It's just a guy in a costume."

"Did you say something to me, Freddy?" asked my mom.

Just then, when I wasn't expecting it, Suzie knocked on the window, and I let out a scream: "AAAAHHHHH!"

Suzie started to laugh. "You are such a fraidy-cat!" she yelled through the window. "Let's go, or all the good costumes will be gone!"

I got out of the car and grabbed my mom's hand. Suzie ran ahead and ran right up to the zombie. I was planning on avoiding him altogether, but then Suzie yelled, "Hey, Freddy, come over here. Check out this awesome costume up close."

I really didn't want to go over there. I wasn't ready to get that close. Not just yet. "I'm sure they have it inside," I called back. "I'll see it when we get in there."

"Whatever," Suzie said.

We all went inside. The place was packed with kids trying on costumes. A princess, a pirate, a ninja, Frankenstein.

"Oh, look, there's Frankenstein," Suzie said. "I hope that means they also have his bride. Let's go look in the girl's section."

"Uh, I'll just stay here and wait," I said.

"Freddy, honey, it's really crowded in here,"

my mom said. "You need to come with us. I don't want to leave you by yourself."

"Oh, I'll be fine. Don't worry about me. I won't go anywhere. I'll just stay right here."

"No, you need to come with us," my mom insisted, pulling me by the hand. "I don't want to lose you."

"Can we go this way?" I asked, pointing in the other direction.

"Freddy, what is wrong with you?"

"I know what's wrong with him," Suzie piped up. "He's too afraid to walk past the wall of masks."

"The what?" my mom asked.

"The wall of masks. That's where they hang all the really scary masks, and you have to walk past it to get to the girl's section."

"I am not afraid of that dumb wall," I said. I really was, but there was no way I was going to let Suzie know that. "I, uh, just don't want to watch a bunch of girls try on silly princess costumes."

"Well, you don't have a choice," my mom said, dragging me down the aisle. "We all need to stay together."

As we walked, we were getting closer and

36

closer to the masks. My palms were starting to sweat. Those masks were so freaky, staring down at us with their evil eyes. My heart started beating faster. What was I going to do? I know. I would just not look at them. I'd keep my eyes on the kids trying on costumes. Pretend to be interested in that. . . .

"Freddy, look," Suzie said, interrupting my thoughts. "How about that one?" She was, of course, pointing to one of the scary masks on the wall.

I just kept walking.

"Freddy, did you hear me?" she said, tapping me on the shoulder. "I said to look at that one that looks like a werewolf. I think you should be that for Halloween."

There was no avoiding it. I had to look at it, or she would never stop calling me a fraidy-cat. I lifted my eyes slowly, took a quick peek, and then quickly turned away. "Nah, I don't like that one."

"You didn't even look at it," Suzie protested.

"Yes I did!"

"No you didn't."

"All right. Enough, you two," my mom said. "Suzie, you need to let Freddy choose the costume he wants, and you choose the costume you want."

"Well, if the fraidy-cat can't even look at a mask without getting freaked out, I don't know how he's going to go to a haunted Halloween party."

"I am not a fraidy-cat!" I yelled at Suzie.

"Freddy, we are in a store," my mom said, putting her finger to her lips. "Please keep your voice down."

"Tell her to stop calling me a fraidy-cat. I am not a fraidy-cat."

"I know you're not a fraidy-cat, sweetheart. Don't let her get to you. You know your sister says things like that just to bother you."

Just then, we rounded the corner to the girl's section. Suzie ran to find her costume, and I finally started to breathe a little easier. At least I didn't have to look at those scary masks anymore. Maybe Suzie was right. Maybe I really was a fraidy-cat. I mean, I was actually afraid of masks. Masks! Just looking at those horrible things made my stomach do flips.

"I got the last one! I got the last Bride of Frankenstein costume," Suzie called as she came running over to us. "I'm so excited. It is the coolest costume."

"Great," said my mom. "OK, Freddy, now it's your turn to look."

"Uh, that's OK, Mom," I said. "I think I'll just be a shark again this year."

"Fraidy-cat," Suzie whispered in my ear as she ran off to pay for her costume.

CHAPTER 4

Big Mouth

Every day at lunch Chloe had been telling us about her big plans for the Halloween party. After all, bragging is what she does best!

"My mom and dad are spending a fortune to turn our house into a real haunted house! Well, *they* aren't actually doing it. They hired these special party planners to set it all up. You are all going to love it. I just can't wait until tomorrow night!" she said, squealing and clapping her hands.

She finally shut her mouth for a second only because she ran out of breath. I guess she never gets tired of listening to herself talk. As soon as she gulped some air, she was off and running again.

"I hope you all have your costumes ready.

You'd better check them and make sure you put them on real tight because we're going to scare the pants off you!" She started laughing hysterically. "Get it? Scare the pants off you? Get it?"

"Oh, we got it," said Max. "It's just only funny when *I* say it."

"Well, nothing you say is going to spoil my party," Chloe said, wagging her finger in Max's face.

"Hey, get your finger out of my face before I bite it."

Max wasn't kidding. He'd already done that once to Chloe. She quickly pulled her finger back. She must have remembered how it felt.

"I can't wait," Jessie chimed in. "I love haunted houses. The scarier the better."

"Good, because this one is going to be super scary," Chloe said.

"Are you going to have dry ice at the party?" asked Robbie.

"Dry ice, ha, ha, ha. That's a good one," Max chuckled. "I thought you were supposed to be some kind of genius, Robbie. Everybody knows that ice isn't dry. It's wet!"

"For your information," Robbie continued, "there is such a thing as dry ice. It's actually what people use to make that sort of creepy fog you see in haunted houses."

Max didn't answer. "Good for you," I whispered to Robbie. "That shut him up."

"Is your haunted house going to be full of monsters?" Jessie asked excitedly. "And how about skeletons in coffins? I love when they pop out of their coffins when you're not expecting it!"

Boy, I wish I could be as brave as Jessie. Nothing and no one seems to scare her. I don't

think she is afraid of anything. I wish I could be like that, but the more she talked about the haunted house, the sicker I felt. I wanted to cover my ears so I couldn't hear what they were talking about, but then everybody would know for sure that I was a fraidy-cat.

"Oh, there's going to be all that stuff," Chloe said. "Skeletons, vampires, mummies, zombies, and even some monsters that jump out at you in the dark or grab your ankles when you're walking through."

"Awesome," Jessie said.

"Are you going to have any games?" I asked. I really needed to talk about something else besides monsters.

"Games? At a halloween party?" Max snickered. "Games are for babies."

"Of course we're going to have games," Chloe said. "We're going to bob for apples, and—"

"Oh, I love that game!" Max interrupted.

"I thought you just said that games are for babies," Jessie mimicked.

"Well, I'm really good at *that* game," Max continued, puffing out his chest. "I always get the most apples."

"That's because he has the biggest mouth," I whispered to Robbie.

Max whipped his head around and grabbed my shirt. "What did you say, Shark Boy?"

"Uh, nothing," I whispered, trying not to laugh in his face.

Max tightened his grip on my shirt. "I know you said something, and I want to know what!"

I gulped. Now I was in trouble. Me and my big fat mouth. "I uh, I uh . . ." I stammered.

"I'll tell you what he said," Jessie butted in. "He said you have a big mouth. A really big mouth. That's why you always get the most apples. Now let go of Freddy's shirt, you big, mean bully."

Everyone started cracking up. Everyone except Max.

Just then, the bell rang, signaling the end of lunch. Phew! Saved by the bell. But before Max let go of my shirt, he whispered in my ear, "You'll be sorry you said that. Just wait until tomorrow night, wimp."

"You are all going to have so much fun at my party!" Chloe sang, as she went to line up.

"I can't wait," Jessie called after her.

"Yeah, I can't wait," I muttered to myself.

CHAPTER 5

Getting Ready

"Freddy, time to come downstairs and get into your costume," my mom called. "You don't want to be late for the party!"

Being late wasn't such a bad idea. Maybe I'd miss the haunted house part and arrive just in time for the games.

"Remember, we promised Robbie's mom that we'd pick him up, so you need to get a move on! Let's go!"

So much for arriving late. I couldn't make

Robbie miss half the party just because I was a fraidy-cat.

But there was no way I was going without my lucky shark's tooth. It always made me feel better when I rubbed it. I had to have it if I was going to make it through that haunted house tonight. My mom was just going to have to wait a few minutes. I had been turning my room upside down searching for it for the last twenty minutes. I sat down on my bed and hit my forehead with the palm of my hand. "Think, think, think." No luck. No good ideas were coming to me. Maybe Suzie knew where it was.

"Suzie!" I called. "Suzie . . . Suzie . . ."

She stuck her head out of the bathroom—that's where she spent most of her time. "What do you want, Stinkyhead? It'd better be something really important. I'm trying to get ready for Amy's party."

I ran over to the bathroom. "Have you seen my lucky shark's tooth?"

"No, and I don't have time to help you look for it." She started to close the bathroom door, but I stuck my foot in before she got it closed all the way.

"Move your foot, you big pain. I told you I don't have time to help you right now. Just leave me alone!"

"But I have to have it for the party tonight, and I can't find it. I really need your help." She was pushing on the door, and it was almost closed. I had to think fast. "If you help me, I'll give you first pick of my Halloween candy. You can take any three pieces you want." After we went trick-or-treating, Suzie and I always dumped out all our candy and spent about an hour trading for our favorites.

"Make it five pieces, and we have a deal," Suzie said.

"Five pieces? That's not fair."

"Take it or leave it." Suzie stuck her pinkie out for a pinkie swear. That's how we sealed all our deals.

"Fine, pinkie swear," I said as we locked our pinkies together.

"Now," said Suzie, "what pair of pants did you wear yesterday?"

"Um, my jeans. Why?"

"Because I bet the tooth is in those pants."

Why didn't I think of that? I had searched all over my room, but I hadn't thought to look in my pants from yesterday. "I think those pants are in the dirty clothes hamper. Let me in, so I can check."

Suzie opened the bathroom door. I ran over to the hamper and started throwing dirty clothes behind me as I looked for my jeans.

"Hey, watch it!" Suzie yelled. I turned and saw that a pair of my underwear had gotten caught in her Bride of Frankenstein wig, which stood about a foot high off her head.

"Sorry!" I said, trying not to laugh. But it looked hilarious.

"It's not funny," Suzie whined. "I spent a lot of time getting this wig on, and now you're messing it up." She gently pulled the underwear off her head.

"Here they are!" I yelled. I had found my jeans. I stuck my hand in one pocket. Not there. My heart sank. I checked the other pocket. Then I felt it. Hard and smooth and sharp. "I got it! Thanks, Suzie," I yelled as I started running downstairs. "You're the best sister in the whole world!"

When I got downstairs, Mom was waiting for me. She was holding the hammerhead costume she had made. It looked really cool.

"This is awesome, Mom," I said. "Just wait till the other kids see this!"

"I'm glad you like it. I've worked hard on

it all week. I think my favorite part is the headpiece. It doesn't cover your face. You just pull it on your head like a hood, and the hammer-looking part sticks off to the sides. Here. Try it all on."

First I pulled on the shark suit that covered my whole body. It was one piece and had a big fin sticking out the back. Then I put on the hammerhead hood. I ran to look in the bathroom mirror. "Cool," I whispered to myself. "Just wait till Max sees this. He won't think it's so lame." Oh no! Max. How could I have forgotten? What was it he said yesterday? "Wait until tomorrow." I was doomed. If I actually survived the haunted house, I still had to face Max. I had already been punched by Max once in my life. I really wasn't looking forward to going through that again.

"Freddy, honey, where did you go?" My

mom's voice interrupted my thoughts. "We have to leave right now. The party starts in ten minutes. Robbie's mom just called. She's wondering where we are."

I took a deep breath and looked in the mirror. "You are not a fraidy-cat," I whispered to my reflection. "You are a big, tough shark."

If only I really believed that!

CHAPTER 6

Enter If You Dare!

As the car stopped in front of Chloe's house, my stomach did a few flips. The party planners she had been talking about every day at lunch sure did a great job. It looked as if we had just pulled up to Dracula's castle.

"This is so cool!" Robbie said as he jumped out of the car and raced toward the door.

"Freddy, honey, don't you want to go with Robbie?" my mom asked.

"Uh, yeah, Mom. I'm just fixing my

costume," I lied. Actually, I was stalling for time. I really didn't want to go anywhere near that haunted house. Just looking at it gave me the creeps.

"Don't worry. Your costume looks great. Have a good time. I'll be back to pick you up at eight o'clock."

I guess I couldn't put it off any longer. I opened the car door and carefully got out, making sure I didn't bump my hammerhead on the roof of the car. "Bye, Mom." I slammed the door and started to walk slowly up to the house. "It's all fake. It's only people in costumes," I whispered to myself. Just then something grabbed me from behind, and I jumped about three feet in the air.

I turned around and saw Jessie smiling at me. "Sorry, Freddy. I didn't mean to scare you. I thought we could go in together."

Walking through with Jessie actually sounded like a great idea since she wasn't afraid of anything.

"I love your costume, Freddy."

"I love your costume, too. You really look like Dracula." Jessie's face was painted white, and she was wearing bloody fangs. Her silky cape was black on one side and red on the other, and she had a little fake bat sewn onto her shoulder.

"Thanks. My *abuela*, you know, my grandma, made it for me. She makes my costumes every year, and she always does a great job."

"My mom makes mine, too."

"Well, let's go," she said, grabbing my hand. "I can't wait. It's going to be super cool."

"Yeah," I mumbled. "Super cool." With my free hand, I rubbed my lucky shark's tooth in my pocket really hard as Jessie practically flew up the front steps, dragging me with her.

When we got to the front door, everyone was already there.

"What took you guys so long?" Chloe whined. "We've been waiting."

"Well, we're here now," said Jessie. "Let's get going!"

A Frankenstein monster appeared in the

doorway and said, "Welcome to Dracula's castle. Enter if you dare."

Oh, why did they have to say stuff like that? It gave me the creeps. But there was no turning back now. I didn't want Jessie to think I was a fraidy-cat. I had no choice. I had to go. I squeezed Jessie's hand tight. The door opened with a CREEEEAAAAAK, and we all followed Frankenstein inside.

That dry-ice fog that Robbie had talked about was swirling around our feet, and spooky music was playing. Next, Dracula appeared and said, "Welcome to my castle. Follow me. I will be your tour guide through this house of horrors." My heart was beating so hard I thought it was going to come out of my chest. "You can do this. You can do this," I whispered to myself.

Dracula led us into a room where there

were skeletons dancing and ghosts floating above our heads.

"OOOOOOOOOOO," Max howled. I was scared enough. I really didn't need his special sound effects.

As we entered the next room, Chloe let out a scream: "AAAAHHHH!"

"What are you screaming about, you little baby?" Max snarled.

"Something . . . just . . . grabbed . . . my . . . leg," Chloe stammered.

"I wish something would grab *my* leg," Max said. "That would be awesome."

I really didn't want anything grabbing me. If I screamed like Chloe, then Max would think I was such a fraidy-cat.

This next room was full of zombies and coffins. Some of the coffins were closed, and some were open. Every once in a while, one of the closed coffins would pop open when you least expected it, and some horrible creature would pop out and make a terrible screeching sound. I couldn't wait to get out of there. Every time one of those things yelled, my whole body shook.

Then Dracula took us into a room where we had to stick our hands in jars and touch

worms and brains and eyeballs. I know the stuff was fake, but it sure felt real. I thought I was going to puke.

"EEEEWWW! EEEWWW! EEEWWW! This is so slimy and gross," said Chloe, shaking her fingers in the air. "I don't want to touch it anymore. I think I'm going to be sick," she said, covering her mouth with her hand. "I

don't want to throw up all over my pretty pink princess dress."

"If you're going to barf, don't do it on me," Max snickered. "Why don't you just leave, and go back to your little tea party?"

"This is *my* party, Max Sellars. You can't tell me what to do!" Chloe huffed.

"Now we are entering the final room,"

Dracula said. "It is my favorite. I want you to meet some of my friends."

"Final room? Did he say final room?" I asked Robbie.

"Yeah, isn't that a bummer?" Robbie said. "I could stay in here all night."

"Me, too," Jessie agreed.

"Not me," I thought. "The sooner we're out of here the better." I was so proud of myself that I had almost made it through without screaming. Now Max couldn't call me a fraidy-cat.

As we entered the final room, something flew right past my head. "What was that?" I whispered to Jessie.

"I don't know," she whispered back.

I ducked, just as another one flew by.

"Don't look now," she said, "but I think one just landed on your shoulder."

I started jumping around like crazy. "Get it off! Get it off!" I yelled.

"What are you screaming about, wimp?" Max laughed. "It's just some stupid, fake, rubber bat," he said, lifting it off my shoulder. "You are such a fraidy-cat!"

So much for making it through the night without screaming.

"That is the end of our tour," Dracula said. "I hope you liked visiting my castle. Please come again."

He opened a door that led out into Chloe's living room where all the games had been set up.

"Oh, bobbing for apples," Max yelled. "I'm first, and I challenge the fraidy-cat over there," he said, pointing to me.

I gulped. I didn't think the night could get any worse.

CHAPTER 7

The Contest

Max ran over to the apple bucket. "Hurry up, Shark Boy," he yelled. "I haven't got all night, you know."

The other kids ran over to the bucket, too, and they started chanting, "Freddy, Freddy!"

I walked slowly. "Why me? Why me?" I thought to myself. "Why couldn't he have picked someone else?" There was no way I could beat Max and his big mouth.

"What's the matter, fraidy-cat?" Max teased.

"You afraid I'm gonna mistake your head for an apple and bite it by accident?"

I gulped. I hadn't actually thought of that. Great! Something else to worry about.

"Oh, he's not afraid of you, you big bully," Jessie said. "Right, Freddy? He's a shark, and sharks are experts in water."

"You'd better take off your hammerhead hood," Robbie said. "It might get in the way. I'll hold it for you."

I took off my hood, handed it to Robbie, and knelt down next to the bucket. The kids started chanting again, "Freddy! Freddy!" I rubbed my lucky shark's tooth.

"Quiet, everyone," Chloe said, stamping her foot. "You have to listen to me. We can't start until I tell you the rules."

Everyone groaned.

"OK," Chloe continued. "When I say 'go,'

you have two minutes to see how many apples you can catch in your mouth. When you get an apple, just drop it on the floor next to the bucket and try for another one. You can't use your hands at all. Only your mouth. Any questions?"

"Yeah," said Max. "When can we start?"

Chloe turned to me. "Are you ready, Freddy?"

"As ready as I'll ever be," I thought. I nodded my head.

"OK, boys, on your mark, get set, go!" Chloe yelled.

I stuck my head in the bucket and immediately swallowed a lot of water. Max's big head was making a lot of waves. I lifted my head to get air and saw that Max had already gotten one apple.

"What's the matter, Hammerhead?" Max said, smiling. "You quit already? I knew you would wimp out. You're such a fraidy-cat."

Now my blood was really starting to boil. I was sick of him calling me a fraidy-cat. I plunged my head back down into the water, grabbed an apple in my teeth, and dropped it on the floor next to the bucket.

"Way to go, Freddy!" Jessie screamed. "That's one!"

Then I heard Robbie yell, "Go for another one, Freddy. Don't stop!"

I stuck my head back in the water and bumped heads with Max. Boy did he have a hard head! Normally I would have started crying, but everyone was watching me. I couldn't stop now.

"That's three for Max!" I heard Chloe yell.

Three? How did he get three already? He

really did have a big mouth! If I was going to beat him, I would have to start acting like a shark. Sharks weren't afraid of anything. Everything was afraid of them. I found another apple, grabbed it with my teeth, and dropped it on the floor.

"That's two for Freddy," Chloe yelled. "There's only one minute left."

Depending on who won, I would be known as the fraidy-cat or the shark. It was now or never. I stuck my head back in the bucket and grabbed another apple.

"That's three for Freddy," Chloe squealed. "It's a tie! Thirty seconds left."

"Come on, *Tiburón*!" Jessie yelled. "You're a shark. Go get him!"

Just then, Max lifted his head out of the water and whispered, "You'll never beat me, you little fraidy-cat."

That was a big mistake. Max lost his concentration, and I dunked my head back in just in time to grab one more apple in my teeth. I triumphantly dropped it on the floor just as Chloe called, "Time's up!"

The kids went crazy cheering for me.

"That was awesome," Robbie said, giving me a high five.

"I knew you could do it," Jessie said, hugging me.

"Here, use these towels and dry off," Chloe said. "You're getting water all over the expensive carpet."

"He must have cheated," Max complained. "There's no way he could beat me."

"He won fair and square," Jessie said. "You're just a sore loser."

"Time for cupcakes, everyone!" Chloe called. "Follow me."

All the kids ran over to the treat table. Everyone except Max. He just sat by himself in the corner and pouted.

"I think Freddy-the-Shark should get the first cupcake," said Jessie.

I grabbed a cupcake and took a big shark bite. Then I smiled a big frosting smile. Maybe the night wasn't so bad after all.

CHAPTER 8

What Was That?

After we finished stuffing our faces with cupcakes, we went to play Pin the Tail on the Werewolf. That's when we heard the noise.

"What was that?" Robbie asked.

"What was what?" asked Chloe.

"That noise."

"What noise?"

"Maybe if you'd just be quiet for a minute, you'd hear it."

We all stood perfectly still and listened.

"EEEOOOWWW . . . EEEOOOWWW."

"That noise," Robbie said.

"I'm sure it's just some spooky music from the haunted house," said Jessie.

Chloe's eyes got big and wide. "I . . . don't . . . think . . . so . . . ," she stuttered. "It sounds like it's coming from down in the basement, and there is no haunted house down there."

Then we heard it again. "EEEOOOWWW . . . EEEOOOWWW."

"I'm scared," said Chloe. "It sounds like a ghost. Do you think it's a ghost?"

"Ghosts aren't real," said Robbie.

"Some people think they are," said Jessie. "My *abuela* believes in ghosts."

"Stop talking about ghosts," Chloe cried, covering her ears. "You're scaring me!"

"You are all such wimps," Max said as he

came over to the group. "I'll go downstairs and check it out."

"All by yourself?" Chloe asked.

"I know none of you fraidy-cats are going to go down there with me."

"Freddy's not a fraidy-cat, remember?" Jessie butted in. "He's a shark, and sharks aren't afraid of anything. He'll go down there with you."

Great! Why did she have to say that? I did not want to go down into that basement with Max, but if I didn't, then everyone would start calling me a fraidy-cat again. I had to go.

"Yeah, right." Max snickered.

I took a deep breath. "Let's go," I said.

Max's eyes almost popped out of his head. "Are you kidding me? You're going to go down there?"

I swallowed hard. "Yep," I said, trying not to let my voice shake.

"Wow! You guys are really brave," Chloe said. "Be careful."

As we started down, we heard the noise again. "EEEOOOWWW . . . EEEOOOWWW." My heart was beating faster and faster with each step I took. What if it really was a ghost? What were Max and I going to do?

We finally reached the basement. It was really dark down there, and we couldn't find the light switch. Luckily there was a full moon, so there was a little bit of moonlight shining in the window.

"EEEOOOWWW . . . EEEOOOWWW." There it was again. What if it attacked us?

"Max, I think the noise is coming from over there," I whispered, pointing to the far corner of the room.

Silence.

"Max," I whispered again, "do you want to go check it out?"

Silence.

"Max?"

I turned around and saw Max frozen like a statue. His mouth was hanging open, his eyes were huge, and he didn't move a muscle. I couldn't believe it. Max, the biggest bully in the whole first grade, the toughest kid in school, was actually a fraidy-cat.

I grabbed his hand, just as Jessie had grabbed mine. "Max, it's OK to be scared," I said. "Everyone gets scared once in a while."

"EEEOOOWWW. . . EEEOOOWWW." The noise sent a shiver down my spine. Max was still frozen. He wasn't going anywhere.

"You stay here, Max. I'll go see what it is."

I tiptoed quietly over toward the noise. I was breathing really fast, and my palms were sweating like crazy. As I got closer, I could tell the noise was coming from behind the washing machine. I bent down and slowly peeked behind the machine. . . .

"Ha, ha, ha, ha, ha!" I started laughing hysterically.

"Hey, stop laughing at me," Max said.

"I'm not laughing at you," I said and giggled. "I'm laughing at this!"

"At what?" Max asked, walking over to where I was.

I held up a small black kitten. "This is what we were all so scared of. This little thing was making all that noise. I guess it got trapped behind the machine and couldn't get out. Let's go upstairs and tell everybody."

Max grabbed my arm. "Wait, Freddy. Tell everybody what?"

"Tell them that the ghost was actually a little kitten."

"Is that all you're going to tell them?"

"Yeah," I said. "Why?"

"So you're not going to tell them about how scared I was?" Max asked.

"Nope. Your secret's safe with me," I said, patting him on the back. "Like I said, even tough guys get scared once in a while."

"Thanks, Freddy," said Max, with a sigh of relief. "I owe you one."

I hid the kitten behind me as we started up the stairs. I wanted to surprise everybody. When we reached the top of the stairs, all the kids were there, anxiously waiting for us.

"Now I'll tell you about the real fraidy-cat," I announced.

Max looked at me in a panic, wondering if I was going to give away his secret.

"Here it is!" I said, pulling the kitten out from behind my back.

"Fifi!" Chloe cried, reaching for the little fluffball. "That's my new kitten. Where did you find her? Tell me the whole story."

"Max and I found her down in the basement trapped behind the washing machine. She must have gotten stuck and was crying so someone would get her out. This little thing was making all that noise!"

"How did you ever get her out of there?" asked Chloe.

"Max and I worked together to rescue her. We were a good team."

"Yeah, that's right," Max said.

"Freddy, you and Max are so brave," said Chloe. "Thank you for rescuing Fifi."

"Oh, it was nothing," I said.

"No problem," said Max.

"There's only one real fraidy-cat in this room," Jessie said, patting me on the back, "and it's a little ball of fur."

"Yep, only one," I said and winked at Max.

DEAR READER,

When I was in second grade, I got the crazy idea that I wanted to dress up as a traffic light for Halloween. My dad worked really hard and made my costume out of a large refrigerator box. He even rigged it with a switch, so that I could actually light up!

On Halloween night, I was so excited to show my friends my cool costume. When I ran out of the house to go trick-or-treating, I tripped down my front steps because I couldn't really see from inside the box. I scraped up both knees and started to cry. My mom cleaned me up, changed me into something else, and my dad wore the traffic light for the rest of the night!

I'm sure you have a great Halloween story of your own. I'd love to hear it. Just write to me at:

Ready, Freddy! Fun Stuff

c/o Scholastic Inc.

P. O. Box 711

New York, NY 10013-0711

I hope you have as much fun reading *Halloween Fraidy-Cat* as I had writing it.

HAPPY READING!

Abby Klein

Freddy's Fun Pages

FREDDY'S SHARK JOURNAL

THE HAMMERHEAD

The hammerhead shark's eyes are on the sides of its head.

It has a sharp sense of smell.

It swings its head from side to side as it swims to pick up smells in the water.

It can pick up small electrical signals given off by stingrays buried in the sand.

Its favorite food is the stingray, and it eats the entire stingray, including its poisonous tail!

HALLOWEEN

Try my fun Halloween picture crossword puzzle. See if you know the names of each thing pictured below and write it in its numbered space going ACROSS or DOWN.

1. ACROSS

8. ACROSS

5. ACROSS

6. DOWN

4. DOWN

3. DOWN

10. DOWN

7. ACROSS

2. DOWN

9. ACROSS

CROSSWORD

DEAR READER,

In Lucky Book Club's October 2005 issue, we asked Ready, Freddy! readers to write about their funniest Halloween memory. We received more than 1,300 entries! Thanks so much for sharing your stories. This one, by Niklaus West of Stroudsburg Elementary School, was selected as the winner—CONGRATULATIONS!

THE FUNNIEST HALLOWEEN EVER

by Niklaus West

The funniest Halloween ever was when my dad played a trick on my mom. It happened two years ago when I lived in East Stroudsburg. My mom is really scared of rats. My dad bought fake rats from the Halloween store so that he could scare my mom. My dad was making a strange noise in the attic to attract my mom. My mom said, "What's that noise?" but nobody answered her. Then she went upstairs and heard the noise coming from the attic. Then she climbed the ladder and looked in the attic. My dad was hiding in a dark corner. He threw a rat at my mom, and she screamed. My mom was so afraid she almost fell down the attic ladder. Luckily, she didn't get hurt. We all started laughing.

Later that night, my mom put makeup on my dad's face while he was sleeping. He had no idea! When the doorbell rang the next morning, my dad answered the door looking like a girl. Everyone laughed, including my mom. She said, "Gotcha!"

Have you read all about Freddy?

 Freddy will do anything to lose a tooth fast!

 Freddy's found the best show-and-tell ever!

Freddy's research turns up some unexpected results!

Can Freddy beat out Max the bully to join the hockey team?

 Help! Does anyone have a magic spell for talent?

Can Freddy find a way to make the vampire go away?

 Yikes! Can Freddy learn to ride a bike in less than two weeks?

Don't miss Freddy's next adventure!